For all my family.

Bloomsbury Publishing,
London, New Delhi, New York and Sydney

First published in Great Britain in 2015
by Bloomsbury Publishing Plc
50 Bedford Square, London, WC1B 3DP

Text and illustrations copyright © John Kelly 2015
The moral right of the author/illustrator has been asserted

A CIP catalogue record for this book
is available from the British Library

ISBN 978 1 4088 5602 4 (HB)
ISBN 978 1 4088 5603 1 (PB)
ISBN 978 1 4088 5601 7 (eBook)

Printed in China by Leo Paper Products, Heshan, Guangdong

1 3 5 7 9 10 8 6 4 2

www.bloomsbury.com

All papers used by Bloomsbury Publishing are natural,
recyclable products made from wood
grown in well-managed forests.
The manufacturing processes conform to the
environmental regulations of the country of origin

Sir Scaly Pants
the Dragon Knight

John Kelly

BLOOMSBURY

LONDON NEW DELHI NEW YORK SYDNEY

Sir Kindly Heart was riding home
from being **bold** and **brave**,
when his horse **tripped** on a **dragon's egg**
abandoned in a glade.

When the egg began to **crack**,
the knight thought, **this looks bad** . . .

But a little **dragon's head**
popped out,
puffed **smoke**,
and **gargled** . . .

"Dad?"

Now since **Sir Kindly** had no child
he took the **dragon** home
and asked his **lady wife**
if they could raise him as their **own**.

His scales were **hard**,
his claws were **sharp**,
but **Lady Kindly** knew
that she would **love** him
as her own **however**
big he grew.

They taught young Scaly **lessons**
and the very **first** he learnt,
was that breathing fire was
not allowed
(in case someone got burnt).

They packed the little fellow off to **Knight School** in a wagon, with **fingers crossed** that no one would be **beastly** to their dragon.

Three **nasty** student knights
– who liked being **mean** and **cruel** –
did **everything** they could to
make it hard for him at school.

They picked the nickname Scaly Pants
and tried to **bully** him.
But words, like arrows, **bounced** right off
his thick green **dragon skin**.

He **studied hard** for many years . . .

learnt how to **ride** and **fight**.

Till he graduated as
the one-and-only . . .

Dragon
Knight!

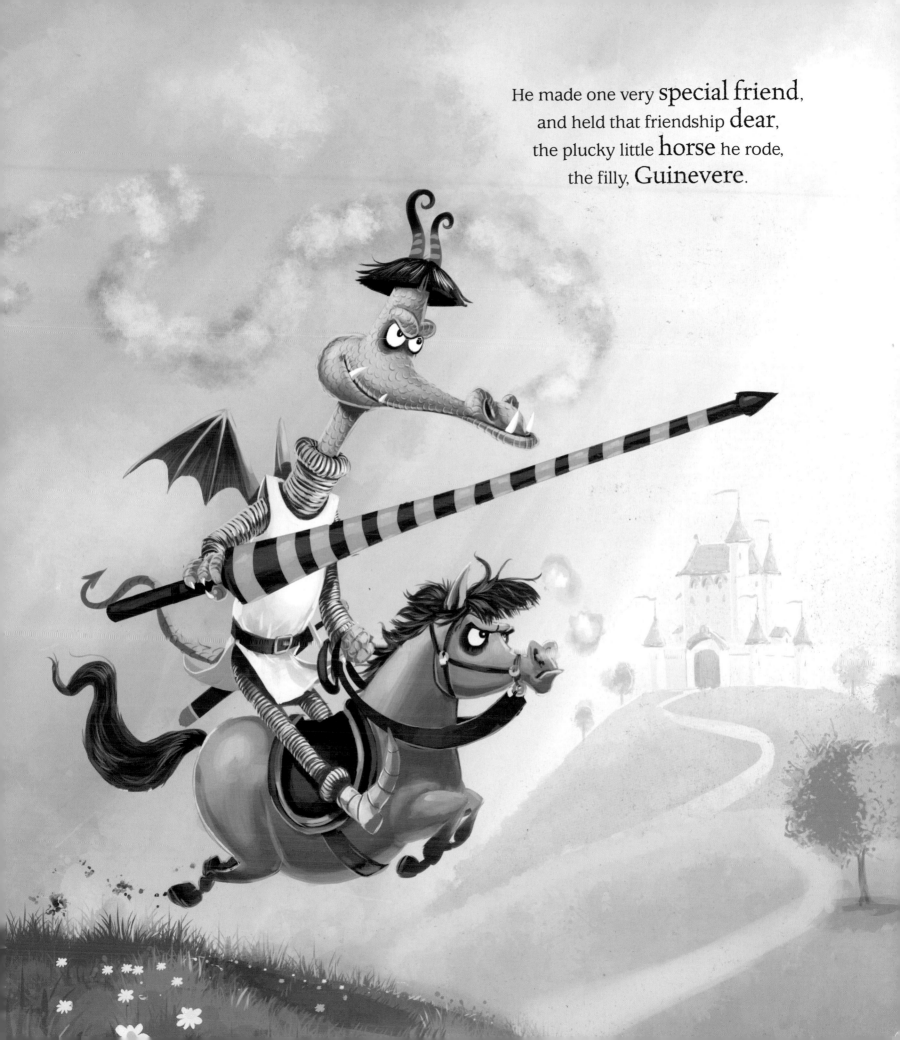

He made one very **special friend**,
and held that friendship **dear**,
the plucky little **horse** he rode,
the filly, Guinevere.

One day a ghastly **giant**
chanced upon their peaceful land.
He **stomped** through town
(knocked buildings down),
grabbed cows in either hand.

He **stuffed** his pockets full of geese,
drained barrels dry of beer,
ate anyone who crossed his path,
and burped . . .

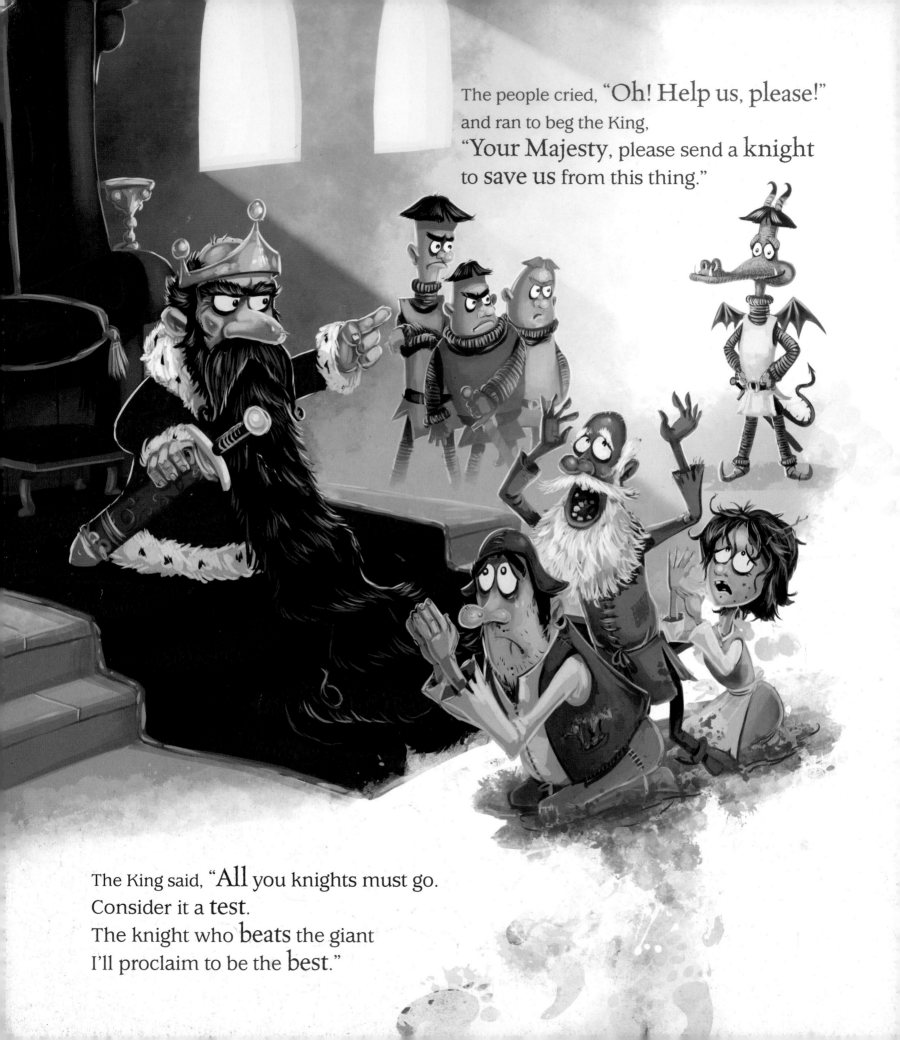

The people cried, "Oh! Help us, please!"
and ran to beg the King,
"Your Majesty, please send a knight
to save us from this thing."

The King said, "All you knights must go.
Consider it a test.
The knight who beats the giant
I'll proclaim to be the best."

The **Nasty Knights** raced on ahead,
each on a **mighty steed**,
with Scaly trailing *far* behind
(at a somewhat **slower** speed).

When he arrived, the **Nasty Knights** were tied tight to a tree.
They stopped their blubbing and cried out, "Oh, Scaly, set us free!"
They begged him, "Don't forsake us! We've **always** been your friends.
Please don't leave your pals to such a **ghastly, gruesome end.**"

The Giant **stomped** towards him.
Its breath was **rank** and **rotten.**
Its red beard **filled** with bits of food
from dinners **long** forgotten.

It bent down, **belched**, and picked a pound of **bogey** from its nose.

He **flicked** it at Scaly, scoffing, "You're the **hero**, I suppose?"

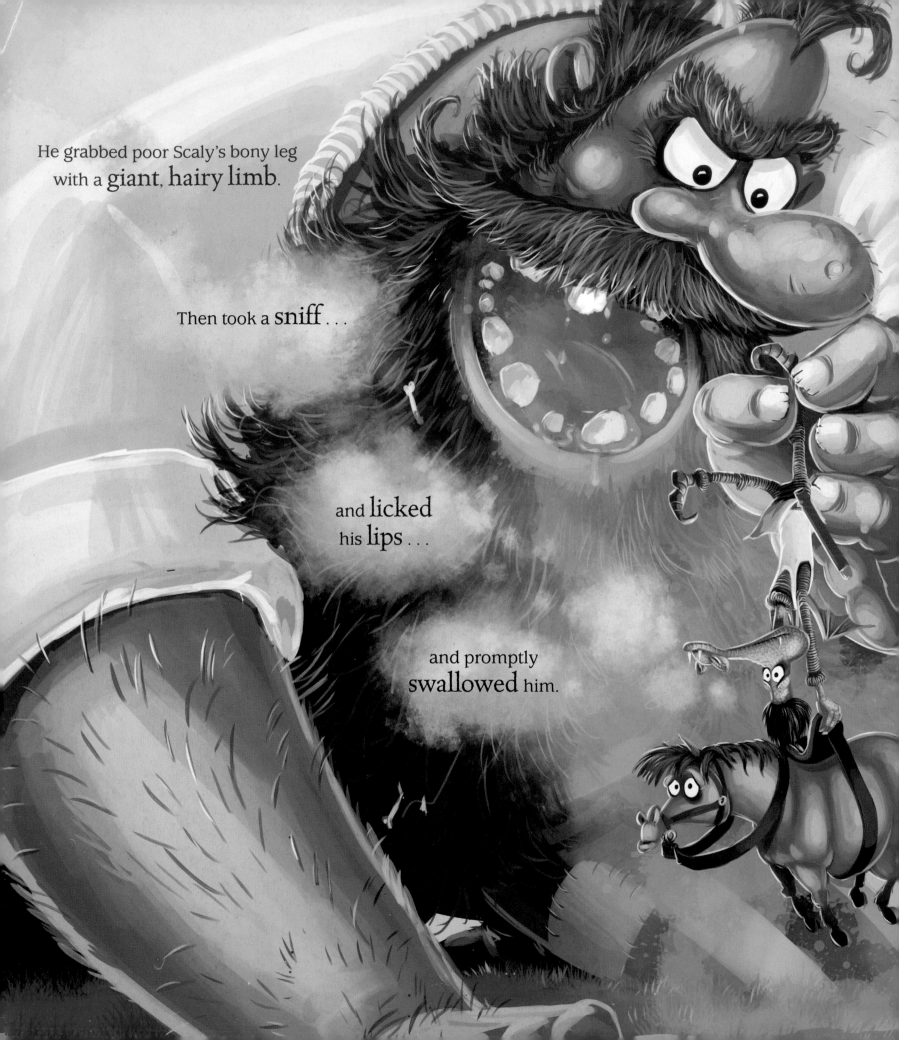

He grabbed poor Scaly's bony leg
with a giant, hairy limb.

Then took a sniff . . .

and licked
his lips . . .

and promptly
swallowed him.

But **Gwinny** ran to **save** him,
and, between the giant's feet,
she found the **sword** that Scaly dropped
and **grabbed** it with her teeth.

She **jabbed** the giant in his **toe**.
He **jumped** and gave a **shout** . . .

. . . his **slimy** mouth gaped open **wide**
and Scaly **plopped** right out.

As Scaly fell he **grabbed** a rope
– and – what a stroke of **luck!**

It was the one that held the
giant's **stinky trousers up**.

Like a circus tent **collapsing**,
his trousers hit the **floor**.

And with a blush, he pulled
them up, and shouted,

"This means war!"

He **chased** them to the edge of town –
they **nearly** got away.
But when Scaly yelled,
"Go faster, Gwinn!"
she fell and panted, "Neigh!"

Scaly drew his **sword** and stood there ready to **defend**,
but the giant **swatted** him away and **grabbed** his little friend.

"I wish I'd time," the giant said,
"to **grind** her bones for bread,
but the chase has left me **peckish**
and **it's time that I was fed**."

His mouth was gaping **wide** and **dark**.
This is it! thought Gwinny.
She put her head between her hooves
and gave a little whinny.

But Scaly wasn't beaten.
There was **one last thing** to try.
He **knew** Mummy wouldn't like it,
but his best friend **couldn't** die.

He drew the **deepest breath** he could,
and **carefully** took aim.

Then **blasted** out a never-ending stream of **dragon flame.**

"Me **bum's** on **fire!**"

the giant shrieked.

His **underpants** were **smoking.**
And since he hadn't **washed** for months
the **smell** had Scaly **choking!**

The giant **leapt** into a lake,
which turned to **clouds** of **steam**,
then **legged** it sharpish from the Realm,
and **never more was seen**.

The news of Scaly's triumph
quickly spread throughout the land.
Till he knelt before the king
who stood with regal sword in hand.

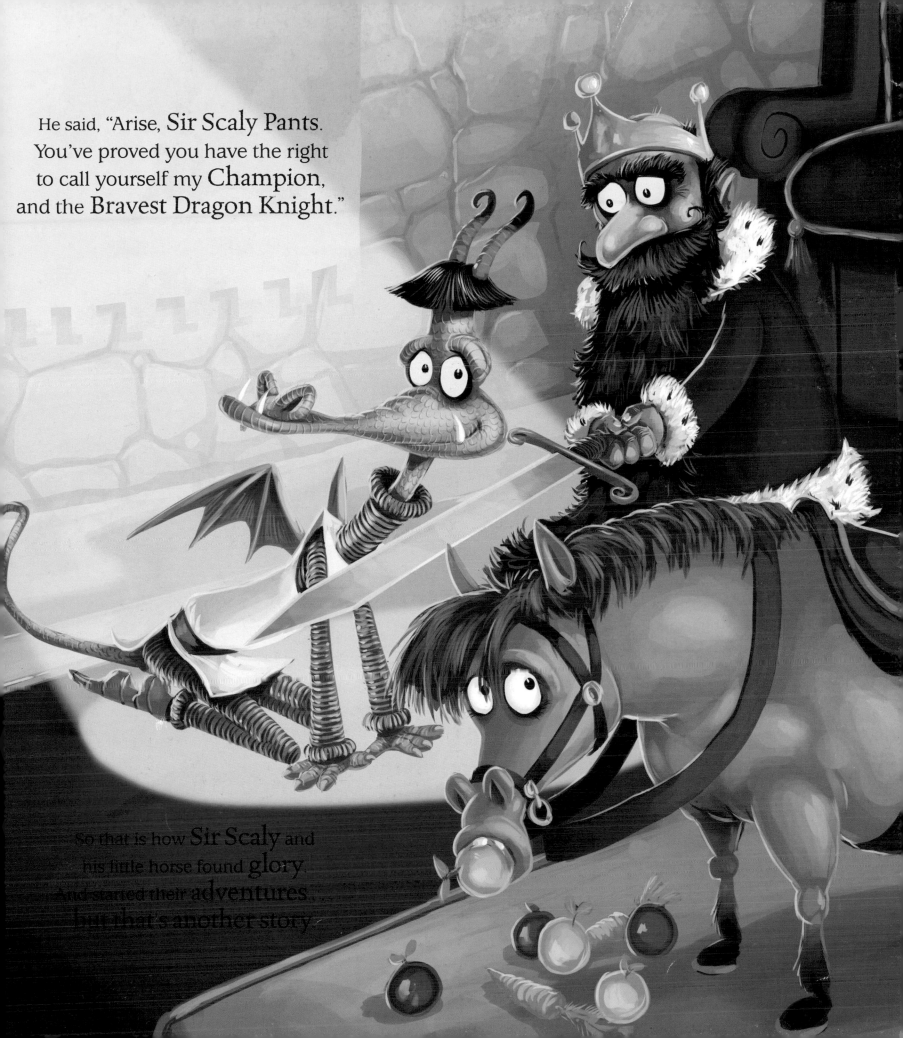

He said, "Arise, Sir Scaly Pants. You've proved you have the right to call yourself my Champion, and the Bravest Dragon Knight."

So that is how Sir Scaly and his little horse found glory. And started their adventures... but that's another story.